THE

# LAST
## *Letter*

# THE
# LAST
# *Letter*

## KIMERLY ROBERSON

AuthorReputationPress®
Creativity & Branding

**Author Reputation Press LLC**
45 Dan Road Suite 5
Canton MA 02021
*www.authorreputationpress.com*
Hotline: 1(800) 220-7660
Fax:      1(855) 752-6001


Ordering Information:
Quantity sales. Special discounts are available on quantity purchases by corporations, associations, and others. For details, contact the publisher at the address above.

Printed in the United States of America.

ISBN-13:   Softcover      978-1-64961-114-7
           eBook          978-1-64961-115-4

Library of Congress Control Number:  2020916761

# DEDICATION PAGE

To the love of my life, my best friend and husband Bill.
Thank you for always having my back and believing in me.

# REUNITED

*Years ago I knew you*
*It seems so long ago*
*When I was young as you were too*
*All those years before*

*As if you never left me*
*You never left my side*
*As if time never passed us*
*But oh the time did fly*

*I miss the way it was*
*When it was you and I and them*
*But I love how it is now*
*When it is you and I again*

Mandi D. Nelson

# Chapter 1

Southeastern Coastal Mountain Range
Collingsfield.
August 18, 2017 7:00 pm

L ily Reid smiles to herself as she checks the email one last time before hitting send. She grabs her keys and purse as she heads out the door to her car. She thinks about her best friend, one of only two people she considers friends, - Katie Dylie, the pretty blonde with blue eyes who lived two doors down from Lily on Medley Street most of her life. She remembers a night twenty years ago as if it was yesterday. It was a hot, day in June 1997 and she had just moved to Collingsfield two months earlier when her dad's company had transferred him. So far she had only met one person her age that she really enjoyed hanging out with. Now, sitting in her driveway twenty years later she reflects on Katie. They had spent every minute of that summer together hanging out at Sterling Lake. She lets the top down on her car in the warm summer night, and stares up at the star filled sky remembering the first time she had met the only other person she considered a friend-- Mike Houghton.

It was August 17, 1997; the night before she was to start her senior year at Collingsfield High School-home of the Collingsfield Mavericks. There was a bonfire at the lake to celebrate the end of summer freedom and Katie had insisted they go, so half-heartedly Lily had agreed, making a promise to herself that she would only stay for a little while, then make some excuse and leave. Lily absently followed Katie around the rowdy party goers faking interest for well over an hour when she noticed a group of guys playing football. She watched for a few minutes noticing one guy in particular as he yelled "go long". He threw the football to another who caught it just as two more tackled him. Lily saw the thrower was a tall guy with dark brown hair. He was cute but not really her type, not many were. She had never had a boyfriend, or many friends for that matter, because she had been told she was weird on several occasions. At least Katie didn't seem to mind, for now. Lily walked down to lake's edge and sat down. Leaning her head back she stared up at the most beautiful star filled sky she had ever seen.

The car's door chime brings Lily's mind back to the present and she turns the key in the ignition, puts the car in drive and turns out onto Melody Drive. She glances at the car's radio clock-- It was 7:15. She wants to stop by the lake for a few minutes before heading to work. If she hurries she'd make it to the The Summit by 11:00. The Summit was the four star restaurant/hotel at the top of Sterling Mountain. The view from every room was amazing, looking out at the mountains on one side and the valley on the other. The first time Lily saw it she knew she wanted to either live there or at least work there so she could see that view every day. She had started right out of high school as a maid and worked her way up to manager of the whole place within six years. It is 7:30 when she gets to the lake. She parks her car, turns off the ignition and gets out. She walks to the water's edge and sits down. She lets her mind drift back to the first day of her senior year when she literally ran into Mike for the very first time.

It was August 18, 1997 and it was an extra hot day. She was standing outside of Collingsfield High School waiting on Katie when someone ran into her, knocking her to the ground. Before she could say anything she heard screaming and felt hands grabbing her arms pulling her up:

"Are you ok?' a male voice asks.

"Of course she's not! You jerk! You ran into her!" Katie screams.

"It was an accident Kaite" the male voice says.

2

"I'm fine" Lily says "But you really don't need to be running down the …the…" she says as she looks up at the same cute dark haired guy from the night before. She tries to regain her voice and tries again. "You really shouldn't be running down the sidewalk" she finally says.

"Right, Sorry about that. I hope you're ok. Who are you anyway?" He says.

"She's Lily Reid. She moved here a couple of months ago. Now go away." Katie growled.

Mike smiled and walked away, but turned around and said "Nice to meet you Lily Reid and Sorry again. Maybe I'll see later".

Katie turned to Lily and asked "Are you O.K.?"

"Yeah, I'm just embarrassed. Who was that?" She said.

"Oh, just Mike Houghton. The school jock and the most eligible bachelor in school. He lives on Empire Street." Katie said

"The most eligible bachelor huh? He doesn't date?" Lily questioned

"Nope! And plenty of girls have tried." Katie said.

"Why not?" Lily asked

"I don't really know. He says he doesn't find anyone really interesting enough" Katie explained.

Lily remembers that first day in bits and pieces. Katie filled in the gossip about the who was dating who, who wanted to date who, which teacher to take and so on until Lily just turned on her mind to auto pilot. It was lunchtime when she finally started paying attention again but only because Mike came to their table and asked if he could sit down.

"Excuse me" Lily asked

"Can I sit down" Mike asked "or are you saving this seat for all the other guys who will want to take you out?'

"Doubtful there will be any other guys so go ahead and sit down" Lily said. And at that moment Lily Reid's life would forever be changed.

Lily's mind comes back to the present and she gets ups and walks back to her car. She gets in, puts the key in the ignition and turns it. She looks at the clock on the radio and notices it is 10:30pm. If she hurries she'll make it to The Summit on time. She puts the car in reverse and heads up Forest Street to Summit Road. She's traveled this road a thousand times so as she enters the curvy entrance she speeds up. On the third turn she skids into the gravel on the side of the road and loses control. As her car heads toward the edge she looks at the clock on the radio. It says 10:45 pm. She smiles and says "Maybe just a little" as her last thought drifts to Mike.

# Chapter 2

New England
August 18, 2017

Mike Houghton was just about to log off his office computer for the day to go meet Sara Brand, his fiancée for dinner to discuss their wedding plans when his notification alerts him to a new email coming in. "Whatever it is can wait until the morning" he said. Then he notices the sender's name: Lily Reid. Quickly he clicks to open the email and reads it.

> *Hi Mike, Hope this doesn't find you too busy. It was great talking to you the other night. I'm glad you are doing well and I'm glad you are happy. Sara sounds like a great girl. I hope she knows how lucky she is…I didn't. Be happy Mike! I don't want you to worry about me Mike. I'll be good from now on. I will always love you. Good bye Mike. Lily*

Mike debates whether or not to reply but as he looks at his watch he notices it is 7:05 and decides to wait until tomorrow to reply so he won't be late meeting Sara. As he logs off and grabs his coats he says "Talk to you tomorrow Lily". He reaches his car, puts his key into the ignition, turns it and opens the sun roof. He glances up at the star filled sky and Lily's face comes to mind. Briefly he remembers a summer night with her by Sterling Lake. The blue water looked almost black in the full moons light. "Get going Mike. You don't want to be late and make your future wife mad" he says to himself. He puts the car in drive and pulls out of the parking garage at 7:15. It's 8:00 when Mike reaches the restaurant and he doesn't think of Lily again until he gets home at 10:30. The last time he talked to her before her last email was two days ago when he had called to tell her he was getting married. She had not been happy. He could understand her being upset. They had talked about getting married once but it hadn't worked out. He would call her tomorrow. It was apparent by her email she wasn't mad anymore and he did love her, he always had, he always would. While Sara wasn't Lily, who was shorter with reddish- blond hair and gorgeous green eyes, Sara was taller and slimmer with brown hair and gorgeous blue eyes, he did enjoy spending time with her and he did love her too. He had to admit, as he got ready for bed, that Sara's eyes were the first thing he had noticed about her 4 years ago. He had only known one other person with gorgeous eyes–Lily Reid and her green ones.

Mike replays her email in his mind as he lay in bed. He was glad she didn't seem upset over their conversation two days ago. He had been really nervous about giving her his news. Once upon a time he would never have dreamed he would be telling her he was marrying someone else. As he falls asleep he remembers the day Lily Reid literally fell into his life. It was August 18, 1997. It had been exactly 20 years ago today. How could he have forgotten! It had been the first day of his senior year at Collingsfield High School. He was running down the sidewalk to meet his friends when he ran right into the most incredible girl he had ever seen and accidently knocked her flat on her ass.

He grabbed her arms to help pull her up as Katie Dylie, screaming, came running up.

"Are you ok?' he asked.

"Of course she's not! You jerk! You ran into her!" Katie was screaming.

"It was an accident Kaite" he said

6

"I'm fine" the girl said "But you really don't need to be running down the …the…" she said. But he didn't hear anything else she said because when she looked up all he saw was two of the most beautiful green eyes he had ever seen.

"You really shouldn't be running down the sidewalk" she finally said.

"Right. Sorry about that. I hope you're ok. Who are you anyway?" he had asked

"She's Lily Reid. She moved here a couple of months ago. Now go away.' Katie growled.

Mike remembered smiling and walking but turning around and saying "Nice to meet you Lily Reid and Sorry again. Maybe I'll see later".

Mike remembered going through that day like it was any other day at Collingsfield High as the star jock. Being patted on the back, girls asking him out, promising him all kinds of things, but all he could think of was her, Lily Reid. Before he knew it, it was lunch and all he could remember wanting to do was getting to know her. He walked up to her table and said "Mind if I sit down?"

"Excuse me" Lily had asked

"Can I sit down" Mike asked "or are you saving this seat for all the other guys who will want to take you out?"

"Doubtful there will be any other guys so go ahead and sit down" Lily said.

And at that moment Mike Houghton's life would forever be changed.

# Chapter 3

Mike's dream changes and he begins to toss and turn. Now he is in a convertible looking out at Sterling Lake. The silhouette of a woman is walking toward the car. When she is close enough he can see it is Lily. As she gets into the driver's seat and starts the car he says "Hi Lily", but she doesn't answer. He watches as she gets in, puts the key in the ignition and turns it. She looks at the clock on the radio and so does he. It says 10:30pm. He watches as she puts the car in reverse and heads up Forest Street to Summit Road. "Lily what are you doing?" he asks her. He realizes she seems to be going faster. "Slow down Lily, You know this road is dangerous" he almost yells. Lily doesn't answer him. She doesn't even seem to notice him. She just stares straight ahead. As she enters the third curve her wheels hit the gravel and she skids. Mike yells "What are you doing?" as the car heads toward the edge. She loses control. As her car heads toward the edge she looks at the clock on the radio, Mike looks at it as well. It says 10:45 pm. "Lily slow down! Are you crazy!" Mike screams at her in his dream. She smiles at him and says "Maybe just a little."

Mike jerks awake to the sound of what he thinks is the sound of glass breaking but realizes it is his phone ringing. He looks at his clock. It says 1:00 am. He grabs his phone and says "Hello".

"Mike, its Katie Dylie. Remember me, from school? Lily's friend" The voice on the other ends says.

A vague awareness hits Mike as he answers "Oh yeah, Hi Katie, why are you calling me at this time of night?"

"I have something to tell you. It's about Lily." She says.

"Yeah, Ok. What about her Katie. Is she alright?" He asks

"No Mike. She's not. She had a car wreck late last night." Katie explains

"What?" Mike says, sitting up abruptly "I don't understand. She emailed me earlier. I, she…" he says, suddenly remembering his dream.

"I'm sorry. I got your number off her computer." She says

"This is insane" He replies

"I know Mike. Her car ran off the edge of Summit Road. It really doesn't make any sense. She drove that road all the time. She knew how dangerous it was. Police said she had to be speeding Mike." Katie explains

"Do they have any idea what time this happened?" Mike asks, not really sure he wanted to know the answer

"As far as they can guess it was between 10:45 pm and 11:15 pm last night. But they really don't know for sure. A couple found the broken fence on their way back from The Summit around 11:30 and they called the police." Katie says "I got the call about midnight".

"Katie I gotta go. I'll be on the first flight I can get on. See you soon." Mike hangs up the phone and sits up on the side of the bed, in complete disbelief.

How could Lily be gone?

Mike's head is spinning and he feels as if he can't breathe. He's confused. How could he have a dream about Lily, a dream about her driving on Summit Road, about her speeding and skidding toward the edge and now her be gone? This couldn't be happening! It just couldn't be! He was still dreaming and any minute he'd wake up. He had to. Lily couldn't be gone! She had sent him a message only a few hours ago. "No I'm wide awake!" he finally says out loud. Knowing he'll never be able to fall back asleep he walks into the kitchen to make a pot of coffee and schedule a flight back home to Collingsfield. After Mike books his flight he calls his office and leaves his secretary a message to clear his schedule for the next week. He gives her the generic excuse of "going home for family business and I will check in later" and hangs up the phone. His next debate is an internal one-whether or not to wake up Sara at 1:30 in the morning to tell her he was going to fly home for the death of his first love, the woman he never told her about, the woman who changed his life. Finally, he decides he'll call her after he arrives in Collingsfield, at least that way he'd have longer to think of something more to tell her about Lily Reid. With that settled he goes back to his bedroom to pack and leave for the airport.

The 3 hour flight doesn't give him any new way to tell Sara why he flew home without calling her or how to tell her about Lily, mostly because all he can think about on the plane is Lily. One memory was of the first time he saw her gorgeous green eyes, eyes that had him breathless, that day he had knocked her down. He saw Lily sitting at a corner table in the cafeteria at school with Katie. They were laughing. He made is way over to them and Lily just looked up at him with those gorgeous green eyes. "God she's beautiful" he thought. "Well just make yourself right at home" Katie grunted. "Thanks, I will" he had said. Her eyes were the most brilliant color of emerald green he had ever seen. He remembered she had been really shy that day. No matter how hard he had tried or how many questions he had asked her, she never said more than two or three words to him. But he wasn't giving up easily. He had waited outside after school, after pleading with coach to let him be late to football practice (which had cost him 10 extra laps that day) just so he could talk to her again and convince her give him her number. It had worked but only after making her feel sorry for him for the extra laps. He smiles at that memory. Telling her how he would suffer 20 laps just to get her to talk to him, had finally made her smile and those emerald eyes had sparkled. A voice over the loud speaker saying "The captain has turned on the return to your seats signs" brings his thoughts back to the present. He was landing. Now it was too late, he had to call Sara and tell her something.

# Chapter 4

Southeastern Coastal Mountain Range
Collingsfield.
August 19, 2017 10:00 am

Mike disembarks the plane and makes his way to baggage claim. Once he claims his baggage he weaves his way through the crowd to the rental car counter. Two and half hours after landing, claiming his luggage, and renting his car he is finally sitting in the driver's seat looking at his cell phone and the 4 voice messages from Sara. He knows, without even listening to them, she would be beyond pissed. How was he going to explain this to her? Without further hesitation he dials his voicemail and hits play: 1. Aug. 19, 2017 8 am the automated voice says. *Hi honey, I called the office, Maggie said you called in and said you had to fly home for some kind of family problem. Why didn't you call me? I don't understand. Call me as soon as you get this.* Ok. That wasn't so bad he thought. At least she wasn't yelling at me. 2. Aug. 19, 2017 8:30 am the automated voice says again *Mike, I'm not sure what's going on but you need to call me. I don't really like you running off in the middle of the night. You should have called me.* Ok, now she's starting to sound pissed. 3. Aug. 19, 2017 9:00 am the same automated voice *Ok Mike I'm really getting worried. I feel like you respect Maggie, your secretary more than you do me! At least she gets a phone call! I don't even get one of those and you're supposed to want to marry me!* Yep there it is. She was beyond pissed now. 4. Aug. 19, 2017 10:00 am the same automated voice once again *Ok Mike, I will give you the benefit of doubt that You may be on a plane and cannot call me back right at the moment. But do not for one minute think that I excuse you from running out in the middle of the night without so much as one little phone call to me telling me what is going on. You need to call me as soon as you land and explain to me what is going on!* Ok still pissed but a reprieve. 'Ok Mike suck it up and call her' he says to himself as he dials Sara's number. She answers on the second ring "Mike damnit, you better have a good explanation" she almost yells.

"Hi honey. I do and I'm sorry" He begins to explain "I didn't want to call you in the middle of the night because I didn't want to wake you up".

"Mike, we are getting married. You are supposed to be able to trust me" Sara responds.

"I do trust you Sara. I just didn't want to wake you up and worry you honey" he continues to explain.

"Oh like finding out from Maggie that you had flown off in the middle of the night didn't worry me. Really Mike?" She says.

"I know Sara. I'm sorry. I should have called you. I called you as soon as I got off the plane and got a signal. Please forgive me. It's just that when I found out a childhood friend died suddenly I guess I wasn't thinking straight honey. I'm sorry" Mike says.

"Oh honey, I'm sorry. I didn't know that's why you left. I still think you should have called me but I guess I can forgive you if you promise to never do that to me again" she responds.

"I won't honey. I promise" He states.

"Good. Is there anything I can do? Do you want me to fly out to be with you?" Sara asks.

"No honey, stay there. I'll be home in a few days" Mike states.

"Ok honey. I love you. Call me in a few days" Sara says.

"I will. I love you too Sara" He says as he hangs up the phone.

Mike calls Katie next. "Katie, Its Mike".

"Hi Mike, is your flight in? Do I need to come pick you up?" she asks.

"No. I got a car. I'll meet you at your house in a few hours" he says.

"Ok" she says.

He puts the key into the ignition, starts the car and pulls out of the parking lot. He heads to Medley Street and downtown Collingsfield. About an hour later he pulls onto Medley Street and finds himself pulling up in front of Lily's house. He can't help parking for a few minutes. His mind takes him back to August 1997. It had taken him over a week after that first day to convince Lily to go out with him. He had started eating lunch with her every day, sitting next to her in English and she was even coming to see him play on Friday nights. Within two weeks they were dating regularly. One night in September he'd asked her to the homecoming dance. "I can't" she said "I don't know how to dance"

"Neither do I, but we can go and not know how to dance together. I really want you to go with me" Mike said.

After a few minutes of begging she finally agreed. Just before she got out of the car she leaned over and whispered in Mike's ear "You make me happy" then she kissed him on the cheek. Mike smiled as he remembered. He had gently grabbed both her arms and playfully pulled her back in the car. He turned her around to face him and whispered in her ear "You make me happy too". Then, he gently took her face in hands and kissed her lips, soft but demanding. Moaning, Lily had leaned into him and wrapped her arms around his neck returning his kiss. Her tongue urging his to explore with hers. He didn't know how long he'd held her in his arms that night but he did remember he had not wanted to let her go and he had not wanted to stop kissing her. Eventually, breathlessly he broke the kiss. "As much as I hate to say this you should probably go in now" he said softly. She smiled softly at him and got out of his car, closed his door, stopped on her porch, turned to smile at him again and went into her house. As she left his car that night so long along she had rooted her place in his heart. As he sits there staring at Lily's house he can almost see her standing on the porch steps looking at him. The ringing of his phone brings him back to reality. It was Katie.

"Mike where are you? I thought you were going to meet me at my house?" Katie states.

"I am" Mike replies "I had to make a stop first. I'm outside on the street in front of Lily's house".

"Oh, ok. I'll be there in a minute". Katie replies softly.

Mike hangs up his phone and is standing beside his car when Katie pulls up. She gets out of her car and walks up to Mike, forcing a small smile. "Kind of expect her to come walking out that door, don't you?" Katie asks in a statement.

"Yeah. I can't believe she won't ever do that again" Mike responds.

"I need to go in and find something of hers to take the funeral home. Do you want to go with me?" Katie asks.

"Sure. I wouldn't mind looking around" he replies as they walk up the walk to the front steps. Pausing at the bottom of the steps he says "You know the entire time we were together she never once invited me over here."

"Well I was only over a few times. I don't think she wanted us around her parents" she says as they climb the steps. Katie put the key in the lock and pauses, saying "I thought it was crazy when she gave me a key after her dad died and her mom remarried and moved to Florida. All she said was 'You never know when I might need you to go in for me'. I guess she just felt better knowing I had it".

All Mike could do was offer a slight grin.

# Chapter 5

Katie takes a deep breath and turns the key, pushes open the door and slowly walks in. Mike follows, slowly looks around and follows Katie up the stairs.

Katie looks through Lily's closet while Mike looks at the pictures on her dresser. He sees pictures of the three of them at his football games and the lake, as well as photos of him and Lily at their prom and graduation.

"What do you think about her little black dress?" Katie asks, holding it up for him to see.

His breath catches in his throat as he remembers the first time he saw her in it. It had been at their five year reunion and she had looked incredible in it. "I think that one is a good choice" he replies softly as he picks through her jewelry box. He picks up a pearl necklace, the one he had given her for their graduation and holds it out to Katie. "I think these will look great with it" he states as Katie takes the pearls.

As she walks toward the door she says "I need to go down and look for some papers and check her messages. Take a few minutes and I'll meet you downstairs".

Mike picks up the picture of him and Lily at their senior prom, themed Enchantment Under the Sea, and sits down on the bed as Katie leaves. Staring at the photo he remembers the night as if it had been only yesterday. It was a warm evening in late April 1998 and she had been waiting on the steps of her porch when he'd arrived that night. He had parked the car, gotten out and stared at the most beautiful girl he had ever seen. She walked toward him in a full length emerald green gown, and with her hair pulled back off her face and her eyes appeared even greener. He pulled her into his arms, gave her a deep, penetrating kiss that left both of them breathless and said "You are beautiful".

He took her hand, walked her around to the passenger side of his car, opened the door and helped her in. He closed her door, ran around to the driver's side, got in and reached into the backseat. He pulled up a small box and handed it to her. As she opened it he said "Since you wanted to keep the color of your dress a secret I thought it was best to go with lilies, well the lady at the flower shop thought it would be". Smiling at him she said " Well if I had told you the color you wouldn't have been surprised".

"I guess your right" he said as he placed the corsage on her wrist. "Well I have a surprise for you. I made dinner reservations at the Summit for us. I know how much you love it up there" he stated as he turned the ignition and pulled out onto Medley Street.

"Hey Mike, you ready to go?" Katie yells up bringing him back to the present.

"Yeah be right down" he yells back as he stands up and places the photo back on her dresser. As he walks slowly toward the door he looks around imagining her here in this room. He could almost see her sitting on her bed, phone at her ear, laughing at his stupid jokes. As he moves slowly toward the door he notices an envelope on her nightstand propped against the lamp. He walks over to it, picks it up and inhales sharply as he sees his name written on the front of the envelope in Lily's handwriting. "What the ….." he whispers as he stares at it. "Why would she leave a letter for me?" He wonders.

"Mike are you coming?" Katie yells again.

"Yeah" he yells back as he puts the letter in his back pocket and goes to meet Katie downstairs.

# Chapter 6

M ike and Katie stand outside Lister's Funeral Home leaning against her car. After a few minutes Katie says "That was the hardest thing I've ever had to do".

Sighing deeply Mike replies " Yeah it seriously sucked". He opens the driver's side door and walks to the passenger side to get in. Looking at Katie solemnly he asks "Do you think you could take me to the spot it happened?"

"Yeah sure" Katie replies as she starts the ignition and pulls out onto Main Street. As she turns onto Medley Drive she states "She drove that road every day, twice a day. Why would she sped knowing how dangerous it is?"

Mike doesn't answer as his dream from the night before replays in his mind. Katie turns onto Summit Road and slows a little. As they come out the second turn he can clearly see what lay up ahead----the third turn. As they approach it he notices the tire tracks in the gravel on the side of the road. His dream flashes in his mind again.. Katie pulls the car over, turns off the ignition and says "I've already walked it so I'll just wait here if you don't mind. Don't really want to do it again".

Without a word Mike gets out of the car and walks toward the tire tracks. He notices the tracks seem to curve back toward the pavement and as he continues to walk their path he notices they reappear in the gravel again. This time they head straight toward the safety fence at the edge. "No skid marks! She didn't even slow down" he says to himself. He walks toward the broken fence and looks over the edge. His heart sinks and he feels sick. He sees broken rocks and trees as the dream replays again in his mind. "What in the hell happened Lily? You knew better!" he says as unshed tears build in his eyes.

He walks back to the car and gets in. taking a breath to settle himself he looks at Kate. "Let's go" he whispers. Quietly, she turns the ignition, turns the car around and slowly heads back down Summit Road.

Katie pulls up behind Mike's car. "Well it's been a very long 24 hours. I need to get home, I'll see you tomorrow for her visitation" Katie says.

"Ok" was all Mike could manage as he gets out of her car. He walks to his car and gets in. Just as he is about to turn the ignition the unshed tears he's been trying to hold back break through and he cries deeply at the loss of Lily.

# Chapter 7

Mike wipes his face, turns the ignition and pulls out onto Medley Street. He needs to go to his parents since they would be expecting him after hearing about the accident. A few minutes later he turns onto Empire Street. As he pulls into the driveway of the house he'd grew up in, the house he'd lived in when Lily was a part of his life he silently prays his mom will not want to have a long talk because he really doesn't feel like talking. He gets out of the car and grabs his bag from the seat before walking up to his house. He rings the doorbell and waits.

"Mike, oh my God! We were expecting you after what happened but didn't know when. You should have called us" his mother says when she opens the door. She steps aside so he could enter and grabs him in a hug. "I'm so sorry Mike. She was such a sweet girl. Her father was a little strange though" she says as she let go of him.

Sighing heavily Mike replies "Thanks but not now mom please" as he heads toward the stairs and his old bedroom. All he wanted to do was be alone and lie down for a little while.

"Dinner will be at 6 honey. Your father will be happy to see you" his mother calls out as he climbs the stairs. "OK" is all he is able to reply. Mike stands in the doorway of his old room. Nothing had changed. "Jeez mom you could have at least redecorated in the last 20 years" he whispers.

Setting his bag down he lays down on his bed. All he wants to do is rest his eyes for a few minutes. Before long he falls into a deep sleep.

Mike was sitting in a car looking at a female figure walking back from the lake. When she was close enough he could see it was Lily. As she got into the driver's seat and started the car he said "Hi Lily", but she didn't answer. He watched as she gets in, puts the key in the ignition and turns it. He watches as she puts the car in reverse and heads up Forest Street to Summit Road. "Lily what are you doing?" he asks her. He realizes she seems to be going faster. "Slow down Lily, You know this road is dangerous" he almost yells. Lily doesn't answer him. She didn't even seem to notice him. She just stares straight ahead. As she enters the third curve her wheels hit the gravel and she skids. Mike yells "What are you doing?" as the car heads toward the edge. She loses control. As her car heads toward the edge Mike jerks awake as he hears Lily calling his name. After a few seconds he realizes it is just his mom. Sitting up he calls back "Yeah mom, I'm coming".

He heads to the bathroom to wash his face. He stares at his reflection in the mirror as he thinks about the dream. "Damnit, why am I still dreaming that". He grabs a towel, dries his face and hands and heads down stairs. He goes into the dining room and sees his parents sitting at the table. "How long was I up in my room?" he asks his mom while he takes a seat and begins to spoon food onto his plate.

"About 2 hours" she states as she takes a bite. "You must have been tired" his dad replies. "it's good to have you home son but I am sorry to hear about the accident".

"Thanks dad but if you don't mind I don't want to talk about the accident or Lily right now" Mike says.

"Sure I understand" his father replies. For the next hour and half they participate in small talk about his job, Sara and the wedding. Once dinner was finished Mike takes his plate into the kitchen but before he can wash it his mom comes in.

"Mike honey I'll do that. I know you probably don't want to right now". Handing her the plate he says

"Thanks mom. I have a couple of things to do so I'm going out for a little while. Don't wait up Ok" and he walks out the back door and around the house to his car.

Mike drives to Summit Road and slowly begins the ascent to the top, to where Lily was headed last night. He slows down even more as he enters the third turn. At the top Mike parks in front of The Summit, turns off the ignition and gets out. He walks through the front door to the foyer. To the right is the dining room. Mike stares at the room, which is decorated with burgundy drapes, beige table cloths and beige carpet, which is a perfect contrast to the light wooden walls. Each table is decorated with white pillar candles and a vase of white roses. Diners eat quietly enjoying the soft music. To the left is a small light wooden counter used as the reception desk for the hotel portion. Behind the counter is a young girl who looks to be about 17 or 18 wearing a burgundy coat, white shirt and black bowtie. She smiles brightly as Mike approaches the counter.

"Good evening sir. How may I help you?" she says

"I'm a friend of Lily Reid and I was wondering if I could look in her office for a few minutes" he replies.

"Oh my gosh sir. I'm so sorry to hear about her accident. She was a great boss and everyone here is heartbroken. She'll be missed a lot" the girl stammers as her eyes glisten with unshed tears.

"Thank you. She was and she will be. Can I go into her office please?" Mike quietly asks.

"Well I'm sure no one will really mind so sure. It's the first door on the right" she states as she points down the hallway to the right.

"Thank you. I won't be long" Mike replies as he walks toward Lily's office.

# Chapter 8

Mike walks slowly into Lily's office and shuts the door. He walks over to her desk and picks up a picture frame. He smiles at the sight of him and Lily at their five year reunion. It was July 2003. Mike sits down in Lily's chair as his mind drifts back. It was 7:30 when he pulled up in front of the high school and parked. As he walked toward the steps he looked at the sound of his name. He smiled as he saw Lily standing there waving at him. She was perfect in the red cocktail dress. He pulled her into his arms for a hug and was stunned when she placed both hands on his cheeks and kissed him. Softly at first but more deeply as his shock wore off, probing his mouth with her tongue. His explored hers back and she moaned softly.

She pulled back, smiled and said "I see some things haven't changed".

He laughed softly "No they haven't" he said.

"Shall we go mingle with all the people we didn't mingle with five years ago?" she asked smiling brightly.

"Sure why not" he replied and took her hand. They walked hand in hand into the school's cafeteria and laughed as they saw Katie waving her arms frantically looking like she was trying to land planes. They made their way over her and sat down.

"So Mike how have you been? You look great" Katie says.

"Things are good and I'm good too" he replies while smiling at Lily.

"Let's go dance" Lily says pulling Mike out of his chair.

Laughing Mike says " Back in high school I thought you didn't like to dance"

"No I didn't know how but now that I do I love to dance" Lily responds as she wiggles her hips back and forth. Laughing Mike takes her hand and leads her to dance floor.

"Oh well third wheel again" Katie sighs.

Several hours later, still laughing Mike leads Lily and Katie out to the parking lot. "I'm not ready to go home" Lily states "Let go to Sterling Lake".

Mike says " Ok that's a good idea. Katie you coming?"

"No I'm going home. Some of us have to work tomorrow but have fun" Katie responds.

"Oh we will" Lily yells from the passenger seat of Mike's car. Fifteen minutes later Mike parks in front of Sterling Lake.

Turning off the ignition he asks "So now what?"

Smiling sheepishly Lily gets out of the car and says "Skinny dipping" as she begins to take her dress off.

"What?" Mike exclaims as he too gets out of the car. Looking up he sees Lily has already shed her clothes and is walking to the lake, deliberately shaking her hips side to side as she looks back over her shoulder at him. Laughing Mike begins to undress as she slowly sinks into the water. Running to the water he yells "Geronimo" as he jumps in splashing her.

Surfacing he finds Lily laughing. She swims over to him and puts her arms around his neck. As she leans in for a kiss she stares into his eyes. Taking his mouth she pushes her tongue into his mouth with forceful desire. Mike wraps his arms around her waist as he lets his tongue reciprocate. Lily wraps her legs around his waist as she breaks the kiss. "I want you. It's been way to long" she pants.

"I want you too Lily" Mike groans out.

"Then what are you waiting for?" she whispers as she takes his mouth with hers one more time.

The kiss turns from heated to feverishly animalistic as he rubs his hands up her back to tangle in her hair. As he enters her she moans deeply and digs her nails into his shoulder. For a few minutes he can only stand still and revel in how good she feels.

Lily moans "Oh God Mike you feel so good".

Slowly Mike begins to move her up and down on his hard shaft until she's panting. After a few minutes he backs her a rock and begins to pump inside her faster. "Oh God Lily" he grunts as he feels her tighten around him. As she shudders on him he lets his release fill her. He just holds her closer as they come back down together slowly.

"That was just as amazing as ever Mike" Lily whispers in his ear as she slowly lowers her legs from around his waist.

"Yes it was. Now I'm glad Katie has to work tomorrow and didn't come." he laughs. They swim around for a short time before deciding to sit on the rocks to dry before going home.

A knock on the door brings him back to the present. "Mister are you ok?" the receptionist calls though the door.

"Um yeah. I'll be out in a minute" Mike calls back as he sets the picture back on her desk. Opening the door to leave he turns around for one last look at part of Lily's world. Mike leaves The Summit and drives back to his parent's house.

Once inside he tells his parents goodnight as he walks up the stairs to his room. He sits on his bed and calls Sara, "Hi honey. How are you?" she asks.

"I'm ok baby. Just getting ready to go to bed. It's been a long day. How are you doing?" he replies. After several minutes of small talk he tells her good bye and removes his shoes. As he removes his pants the letter he found at Lily's house falls out of his pocket. To emotionally drained to read it now he places it on the dresser and gets ready for bed. The dream returns.

# Chapter 9

M ike woke the next morning after a fitful night of sleep. He glances at the letter on the dresser but decides the smell of coffee and bacon seeping under thru the bedroom door was a bigger draw. Getting out of bed he made his way downstairs.

"Good morning son" his mother says as he enters the kitchen.

"Good morning mom. Dad gone to work?" he responds.

"Yes but he'll be off early today." She answers.

"Good" he says as he pours a cup of coffee. Sitting at the table he sighs.

"I'll fix you some eggs to go with the bacon" his mom says. As she cooks she looks over her shoulder at him and asks "How are you doing honey? We are so very sorry about Lily's accident. She was such a sweet person."

He looks up catching her looking at him and says " Thanks mom. I still can't believe she's gone. I'll be out taking care of some stuff today but I'll see you tonight for dinner."

"Ok honey" she responds as she places a plate of bacon and eggs in front of him "At least eat breakfast son."

"Ok. Thanks mom" he says as he picks up his fork.

When he's finished eating he returns upstairs and takes a shower. Just as he gets out his phone rings. Picking it up he sees that it's Sara. "Hi honey" he says on the third ring.

"Hi baby. I just wanted to see how you're doing and hear your voice." Sara's voice comes thru the phone.

"I'm good. Just got out of the shower. Got some things to do today before the visitation toight." He tells her.

"Are you sure you don't want me to fly out and be there for you? I can clear my schedule." she replies.

"No honey. I'm ok. I'll be home in a couple of days. I love you Sara." He explains.

"Ok and I love you too." She says and hangs up.

He returns to the bathroom to finish getting dressed and just as he's about to pick up the letter his phone rings again. Sighing he picks up his phone. "Hello" he says. "Mike it's Katie. I'll be at your house in a few minutes. I wanted to see if you wanted to go with me to clean out Lily's office."

"Um yeah. I can do that. See you in a few minutes." he answers.

Hanging up the phone he goes downstairs and tells his mom goodbye. Going outside he sees Katie pull up. She stops in front of the house and he gets in. Pulling out into the road she says "Thanks for going with me. I really didn't want to do this alone."

"No problem" he says and they ride up Summit Road in silence, each in their own thoughts. All to soon it seems Katie parks in front of The Summit and turns the car off. Getting out she sighs "Ok let's get this over with." Mike takes a deep breath and gets out to follow her in. He notices the same young girl from the night before at the front desk and she halfheartedly smiles at them.

"Good morning Katie." she says.

"Well it's morning Brenda but not so good for me but thanks." Katie replies "We're here to clean out her office. Is it ok if we go on in?"

"Yes ma'am. Go ahead. I'm so sorry Katie. She will be missed." Brenda replies.

Katie walks toward Lily's office and Mike solemnly follows. Once inside he notices Katie's eyes show unshed tears. He grabs her in a hug and she lets the tears fall. He just holds her and lets her cry until she's finished and says "I never thought we'd ever have to go through this so soon but here we are."

"I didn't think so either and it really sucks." Katie replies "Let do this so we can get out of here."

As Katie began to box up Lily's things he wanders around looking at photos hanging on the wall. He notices a masquerade mask on the book shelf and picks it up. The last time he'd seen it was May 2008. His mind drifts back to the night so long ago and he's walking across the school's parking lot to his 10 year reunion when he sees Lily standing on the steps wearing the mask. She reaches out to take his hand when he approaches her and he says "I was thinking a masquerade theme was a stupid idea for this thing until I saw you standing here looking all sexy in that mask." he says.

Smiling she said "It was meant to hide my identity from you."

"I'll always know who you are Lily. Nothing can hide that"

Laughing she throws her arm over his shoulder and asks "So where's your mask?"

"Right here" he says pulling his mask out of his coat pocket as he pulled her in for a kiss.

For a few hours they laughed and joked relieving memories while music surrounded them. During the last slow dance of the night she suggest "Let's drive up to The Summit and I'll show the office I worked my ass off to get."

"Sounds good" he replied as the song ends. They say their goodbyes and walk hand in hand to his car. They laugh and engage in small talk about how much some of their classmates had changed and speculated about the ones who hadn't. Once they reached The Summit she turns serious and her mood visibly changes. As he turns off the car he notices she's giving him a seductive smile as she gets out of the car. Smiling to himself he gets out to follow her.

There is no one at front desk and the restaurant is closed but taking his hand she walks to her office anyway. Once inside she closes and locks the door. He looks around and whistles "Wow. You've done good girl. This is nice."

She laughs, raising an eyebrow saying "Well I did work my ass off as a housekeeper then waitress then assistant manager to get this office" she laughs.

He pulls her to him grabbing her ass and says "Well I like the ass it gave you" and takes her mouth with his. She wraps her arms around his neck as she leans into the kiss plunging her tongue into his mouth connecting with his. He groans as he says " Why does just looking at you make me so hard?" and he takes her mouth again, this time hungrily. As she backs him to the couch she begins unbuttoning his shirt. Without breaking the kiss he removes his jacket then his shirt. As he sits down on the couch she straddles him winding her hands thru his hair. "I want to feel you inside me" she moans as she pulls her dress over her head and throws in to the floor.

She captures his mouth again as she reaches for his belt and unfastens it pulling it off and tossing it to the floor as well. He breaks the kiss and sets her on her feet long enough to remove his shoes and pants and pulls her back onto his lap as he sits back down. As she slide onto his hard shaft he notices she's wetter than he can remember her ever being. "OH God your so wet Lily" he groans as she settles herself on him.

"MMMM" she groans as she slowly begins to move up and down on his rock hard penis. He grabs her hips to guide her and as she throws her head back she begins to move faster. Her nails dig into his thighs as her oozing channel begins to tighten around him. As she yells out his name she begins to convulse and he can no longer hold back as he empties himself into her throbbing hole. He pants as she wrings out every drop from his pulsing rod. "Awesome as always" she pants as she kisses him lightly.

"You bet your ass it was, It's always been awesome with you" he replies.

"As she rolls off him to sit next to him on the couch he runs his hands through his hair. As much as I'm enjoying this night I have an early flight to catch. I wish I could stay longer but work calls." He says.

She sighs "I know and I wish it didn't have to end."

Katie calling his name and tapping on his shoulder brings him back to the present. "Hey there big guy. You were far away. I've been calling your name for like 5 minutes. Good memory" Katie states.

"Um yeah. My mind drifted. Sorry" he replies. He and Katie finishes packing Lily's things and make their way back to the car.

Katie states "I'll drop you off and take this stuff to her house. For some reason I feel the need to water her plants."

When Katie drops him off at his house he notices his dad did indeed get off early. As she parks in front of his house she sighs "Well I guess I'll see you at the visitation and funeral tomorrow at 1."

"Yeah. See you then" he says as he gets out of the car. He walks up the walkway and into his house as Katie drives away.

"Hi son" his dad yells from the living room "Your mom says dinner will be ready at 6."

"Ok dad. I'll be in my room if you need me." He yells back as he ascends the stairs. He stops in the bathroom for some Tylenol to ease the massive headache that had developed. He enters his room and looks around. "Why hasn't my mom redecorated this room like every other mom in the world?" he wonders. "I've had enough memories for one day." He decides to go to the backyard for some fresh air and to escape the memories. He doesn't even look at the letter on his dresser.

# Chapter 10

Mike awoke the next morning after another fitful night's sleep but luckily his headache was gone. Dinner last night had been an exercise in his parents tiptoeing around any subject that might include Lily and then a quiet night watching some TV before taking two more Tylenol and going to bed. Now he had to get up and face telling the first love of his life, the green eyed beauty that had changed his life goodbye forever. "Get up and get going. Get this day over with." He says as he heads into the shower. Thirty minutes later, showered, shaved and dressed he walked into the kitchen for a cup of coffee.

"Good morning son. You're dressed awful early for today" his dad states.

"Yeah I want to run a couple of errands before" he answers as he leans on the counter to drink his coffee.

"Well I better go get myself showered and ready. See you later son." His mom declares as she walks out of the kitchen.

Mike finishes his coffee, puts his cup in the sink and walks out to his car. Once inside he calls Katie "Hey Katie I was wondering if I could get Lily's house key from you? I just want to stop by there one last time." He asks.

"Sure Mike I'll meet you there in 10 minutes" she replies.

He starts the car and as he backs out of his driveway his phone rings. He answers on the second ring "Hello".

"Hi Mike. I just wanted to tell you I'm really thinking about you today and I miss you terribly" Sara says on the other end of the phone.

"Hi honey. Thank you and I miss you too but I'll be home tomorrow." he replies.

"Honey I'm sorry about your friend but I want you home' she declares.

"I know you do and I said I'd be home tomorrow Sara. I gotta go. See you tomorrow." he says hanging up the phone in a huff. "Damnit, it's not her fault. Now I have to apologize for snapping at her' he breathes out as he pulls up in front of Lily's house. He sees Katie waiting. "Thanks Katie I just need a little time alone here ya know:" he states as he gets out of the car and walks up the driveway.

"I understand" Katie says as she unlocks the door "Just lock up when you leave" she replies.

Mike closes the door behind him as he enters Lily's house. He slowly looks around.. He can almost imagine her sitting in the living room, standing at the kitchen counter as he walks into each room. Finally he reaches her bedroom and sits down on her bed. He imagines her sitting there laughing with him in the phone, doing homework, sleeping. "What happened Lily? Why? How were your so careless?" he screams as he lets the tears he'd been holding back fall freely. For what seemed like a long time he sat there with the tears falling and the memories flowing until he had no more tears left to fall. He gets up, walks into the bathroom to blow his nose and wash his face. 'One more stop and I'll be ready' he thinks as he leaves her bedroom and makes his way outside to his car. He backs out and heads toward town for that last stop.

# Chapter 11

Mike pulls up to the funeral home at 12:45. After parking he just stares out the window a few minutes before getting out and grabbing the arrangements of lilies from his passenger seat. As he heads in he sees Katie waiting by the front door. "Oh my God Mike. I was getting worried."

"I wanted to stop and get these before I came " he replies solemnly.

He opens the door and holds it for Katie to enter then follows her in. He notices all the people and thinks Lily would be happy to see this many people here. After sitting through the hardest and longest hour of his life he drives to the cemetery behind the hearse. After another hard 30 minutes he's standing by the graveside alone. "I miss you Lily and I will always love you". As he looks up he thinks he sees her standing by a tree smiling her infectious smile at him. He closes his eyes and when he opens them again there's nothing there. "Must be lack of sleep" he thinks as he turns away from the grave and makes his way back to his car.

When he gets home his mom yells "Dinner in 30 minutes son" from the kitchen.

"Ok mom. I'm just going to change clothes" he yells back as he climbs the stairs. In his room he sits on his bed and sighs "Who knew an funeral could be so exhausting" As he gets up to change clothes he notices the letter on his dresser. He walks over, picks it up and sits back down in his bed staring at it. "When did you know I'd be here Lily and when did you write this?" he breathes as he turns it over and opens the envelop. Unfolding the letter he reads: *"Hi Mike. If you're reading this I'm not physically here anymore. I just wanted to apologize for getting mad at you last month when you told me you were marrying Sara. It was jealously and I'm sorry. I know you will always love me just as I will always love you but I also know you are allowed to love someone else. I was wrong to ask you to make a choice on who you wanted in your life. It wasn't fair so I've made the choice for you Mike because I love you. Now I'll always be with you. Good bye Mike."*

"What are you talking about Lily? This just can't be real " Mike states dumbfounded. "Oh Lily, why? Yes I'll always love you".

# Chapter 12

## EPILOGUE

Two years later.

Mike sits on his wife's Sara's hospital bed as she cuddles his brand new baby girl. "She just so beautiful" Sara says with tears in his eyes.

"Yes she is. Just like her momma". Mike states.

"What do you think we should name her?" Sara asks

Sighing deeply Mike replies "Well I've always loved the name Lily".

In the background Lily smiles and fades away.

CPSIA information can be obtained
at www.ICGtesting.com
Printed in the USA
BVHW041713070223
658069BV00021B/225